ONE
VALENCIA
LANE

NEW LOVERS is a series devoted to
publishing new works of erotica
that explore the complexities
bedevilling contemporary
life, culture, and
art today.

OTHER TITLES IN THE SERIES
How to Train Your Virgin
We Love Lucy
God, I Don't Even Know Your Name
I Would Do Anything For Love
My Wet Hot Drone Summer
Burning Blue
Kuntalini

ONE
VALENCIA
LANE

×

BETTINA DAVIS

BADLANDS UNLIMITED
NEW LOVERS
N°8

One Valencia Lane
by Bettina Davis

New Lovers No.8

Published by:
Badlands Unlimited LLC
operator@badlandsunlimited.com
www.badlandsunlimited.com

Series editors: Paul Chan, Ian Cheng, Micaela Durand, Matthew So
Copy editor: Charlotte Carter
Editorial assistant: Parker Bruce
Ebook designer: Micaela Durand
Front cover design by Kobi Benzari
Special thanks to Luke Brown, Rachel Davies, Elisa Leshowitz

Paper book distributed in the Americas by:
ARTBOOK | D.A.P. USA
155 6th Avenue, 2nd Floor
New York, NY 10013
Tel. +1 800 338 BOOK
www.artbook.com

Paper book distributed in Europe by:
Buchhandlung Walther König
Ehrenstrasse 4ß
50672 Köln
www.buchhandlung-walther-koenig.de

Printed in the United States of America

ISBN: 978-1-936440-99-3
E-Book ISBN: 978-1-936440-46-7

www.badlandsunlimited.com

CONTENTS

Chapter 1: Bloody Mary   1

Chapter 2: Metro North   23

Chapter 3: S.D.   47

Chapter 4: Balthazar   67

Chapter 5: Cleopatra's Needle   83

Chapter 6: Fountain   97

About the Author   119

Chapter 1
Bloody Mary

It was one of those sultry August days in the city. No matter what I put on, it felt like too much. I had just taken a cold shower and slipped on a lace mini-dress fresh from the dry cleaners, not caring that I looked like I was heading to the beach instead of an upscale midtown bar.

"It's a scorcher," said my doorman,

Charlie, as I breezed through the lobby of my building.

As soon as I stepped out onto Park Avenue, I felt as though I would suffocate in my own skin. Tiny beads of perspiration dripped down my chest and back. I should have hailed a cab, since I was already running late, but I was in the mood to walk. There was something about strolling down Park Avenue at dusk that always excited me. The closer I got to the MetLife Building, the more the sidewalks bustled. Men in suits sans ties descended into the subway or rushed toward Grand Central to catch the Metro North back to the suburbs. Gleaming black Cadillac Escalades waited at street corners to take bankers and lawyers from their offices to their dinner meetings downtown.

In a white babydoll dress that barely covered my ass, I made quite a spectacle amidst the sea of dark suits. A handsome man in his fifties glanced up from his Blackberry and looked at me. As I walked past him I could feel his eyes tracing my figure.

It gave me a rush to feel strangers watching me. I imagined the man going home to his frigid, tight-faced wife. He would immediately tell her he had a migraine and retreat to the privacy of his bedroom to fondle himself. He would fantasize about me: the smooth, tanned skin of my upper thighs glistening with sweat; my young, supple breasts bobbing beneath my sheer minidress.

My own fantasy life had gotten out of hand since I had quit modeling just a few weeks before. I missed feeling like the center of a man's attention. Womanizing photographers and droves of wealthy men overran the New York fashion world, lurking at parties and events hoping to land a "10" wife, girlfriend, or just a one-night stand. The whole scene had started to wear on me, but it only took a few weeks out of the loop for me to yearn for it again. Maybe I wasn't cut out for real life. Maybe I was better off in a fantasyland of makeup, clothes, sex, and illusions.

But just as I was drifting off into daydreams, the city jolted me back down to concrete and humidity. A cab nearly rammed into me as I crossed Fifty-fifth Street at Madison Avenue. The Sony Tower loomed above me. Midtown was like a vortex. Why had my friend Annabelle wanted to meet at the St. Regis Hotel, of all places? She was probably hooking up with some elderly European guy there for dinner later. That was her type. She liked tourists, because they meant no strings.

I walked past the hotel doormen in their green penguin suits and black top hats. They must have been dying in the heat under those heavy uniforms. Once I set foot in the bright marble lobby, the icebox air and the scent of jasmine overwhelmed me. Fancy hotels always seemed to smell the same. There was a bouquet of white lilies piled high in a gold urn at the foot of the grand staircase. I noticed their deep scarlet stamens quivering in the artificial breeze.

✕

As soon as I entered the King Cole Bar I felt engulfed in its dark woods, lavish décor, and subdued reddish lighting. The oppressive summer air seemed miles away as I settled into a studded velvet lounge chair next to Annabelle, who was sipping a Bloody Mary.

"Hey stranger," she chimed. Annabelle was about to make it big doing swimsuit stuff. Nothing high fashion, because her look, like mine, was too pretty and all-American. Plus, she had great tits, so that didn't hurt. She took a luxurious sip of her thick, red drink.

"I ordered you one," she said. "They're killer. Apparently they're the signature drink here."

"Thanks," I replied.

"So how's life out of the fast lane treating you?"

"It could be worse," I said.

"And the hubby?" she asked, toying with her lustrous platinum hair.

"Landon is fine," I said. My cocktail arrived just in time. Talking about my husband was not the high point of any conversation. I took a sip of the peppery, vegetal drink. It was like an elixir to soothe my whirring mind and tense muscles. I wondered where Landon was at that very minute. It was seven o'clock, so he was probably ordering sushi for dinner and working on some complicated legal brief. His office was just a few blocks away in the gleaming marble GM Building that overlooked Central Park.

"You guys had the most drop-dead

gorgeous wedding," Annabelle said. "You can't be disappointed already. I didn't spend a grand to go to Martha's Vineyard for three days just so you could get divorced a year later."

I was just a few weeks away from my one-year anniversary. Landon had charmed me with his old-fashioned manners and his almost nerdy dedication to his work in corporate tax law. He was always reading, whether it was the tax code, the *Wall Street Journal*, or even Shakespeare. I preferred real-life action over secondhand experiences from newspapers and books.

"I'm not disappointed," I finally said, after savoring another sip of my Bloody Mary. The cayenne pepper and horseradish tingled and burned.

"If you're so bored, why don't you get pregnant already? Doesn't Landon want to have a whole gaggle of preppy kids?"

"I'm not ready," I said. "I don't know if I'll ever be ready for that."

"Oh, come on," Annabelle snipped. "You have this hunky Boston Brahmin husband from the perfect family who makes half a million dollars a year. Plus, he's a sweetheart. I'd kill for your life. You think I want to be dieting and running around the city all day with obnoxious casting directors poking at me and calling me fat? I'd trade lives with you any time."

"You're not fat," I said.

"I know," Annabelle replied. "I'm just tired of the bullshit, and I'm only twenty-three. I'm too young to be tired." She fidgeted with the St. Regis swizzle stick in her drink. Her iPhone buzzed with a new message, immersing her in a flurry of texts. She always had at least a handful of guys after her. I didn't miss the frustrations of dating and playing games.

The problem was that my married life without modeling totally bored me. I had been the bad girl of my New England boarding school. As a senior I would sneak out of my dorm after check-in and hook up with my boyfriend in the back of the chapel. I had to do something to entertain myself while not trapped in Latin class or on some playing field. After graduation I had convinced my parents to let me take a year off before college to live in Manhattan. They thought I was interning at Sotheby's, but I was actually plunging as far down the rabbit hole as I could. Ten years had gone by, and I hadn't changed. I wasn't the prissy Park Avenue housewife, just as I hadn't been the overachieving prep school student. I felt bored stiff and craved my next escape.

Annabelle finally looked up from her iPhone.

"Don't hate me," she said. "I have to go in, like, ten minutes. This new guy, Ray, is totally ridiculous. He wants to meet me at eight in Brooklyn. Apparently there's some new Japanese-Jewish restaurant that all his friends have been raving about. His car is picking me up soon." She checked her makeup and pulled her wallet out of her new Chloé satchel.

"No no," I said. "It's my treat. Plus,

I think I'm going to stick around for another one. Suddenly I feel so relaxed."

"You're the best," she said, leaning in to kiss me on the cheek.

As soon as Annabelle left, I checked my phone to see if Landon had texted me. He had: I'll be home at 9, can't wait to see you! I immediately felt guilty for even suggesting to Annabelle that I wasn't madly in love with him. But the truth was that there was something missing, and the more time that passed, the more I felt an emptiness swelling deep inside me.

Just then, my waiter came over with a second drink.

"Compliments of an admirer," he said, setting down the Bloody Mary in front of me.

"Okay," I replied, confused. I took a sip of my new drink, savoring it all the more because it had come from the generosity of a mysterious stranger. All of a sudden I felt the presence of someone behind me. The scent of cologne wafted through the air: something exotic with hints of black pepper and coriander.

His thick, muscular hand touched my shoulder. He leaned over and placed a business card on the table next to my drink. But when I turned to see his face he disappeared into the crowd. All I saw of him was his hulking frame. He must have been close to six-foot-six. He had wild dark hair and was wearing a navy linen suit that looked custom made.

I snatched up the card that he had left behind. It had a gold sheen to it and was on thick paper. Instead of a name and an email address or a phone number, a street address was printed across it in small, antique typeface: One Valencia Lane, Bedford, New York. That was all.

Was someone playing an elaborate prank? Had one of Annabelle's beaus helped in some silly plot she had concocted to amuse me? I hoped it was more than smoke and mirrors. Something about the heavy gold calling card felt too serious to be part of a joke.

×

Back in the master bathroom of my apartment, the stark white tiles and bright lighting made the hazy atmosphere of the St. Regis feel like it had all been a dream.

I got into the shower, lathered my

body with soap. I felt dirty after being out in the streets of New York City. I went over the events of the evening in my mind, trying to remember more details about the mysterious man. Something about him stuck in my memory. As I thought about him, I slid my hand across my smooth, tanned stomach, making my way down to press my fingers against my clit. I spread the lips apart as I stroked my pussy, imagining what it would be like to be single again. To be Annabelle. I could go home with any guy I wanted. I wondered what it would be like to leave the St. Regis with the mysterious stranger. To follow him back to his apartment, or his hotel room, where I would let him turn me around, push my dress up above my ass, roughly slide my panties down while he fucked me hard against the wall and then left me begging him for more. My mind drifted back to Landon, who was due home at any moment. I wished he would be rough with me. I longed for him to find me in the shower, to push me up against the tile and bend me over, fucking me deep, filling my pussy until it was dripping with his cum. I wanted him to punish me for being a naughty girl— for thinking of other men like the dirty slut that lurked inside me.

"Greta," my husband called. "Where are you?"

"In the shower," I said, slipping my fingers out of my pussy and hoping he would read my mind and come into the bathroom to have his way with me. Then I remembered the reality of our marriage.

As much as I loved Landon, he wasn't spontaneous or wild, and he certainly wasn't the type to take charge of a sexual situation. In some way, I suppose, that's why I'd married him. I was tired of being used by all the photographers, the directors, and the producers. I wanted somebody who would take care of me and love me for who I was.

As I came back to reality, I rubbed a towel over my damp skin and headed into the bedroom. The closet door was open and Landon was taking his suit off. I dropped my towel on the floor and crept in behind him, pressing my naked body up against his back. Still aroused, I slid my hand down to his waist and felt for his penis.

"Wow," he said, turning around to

give me a kiss on the lips. "What got into you?"

"Nothing," I said. "I'm just feeling very . . . relaxed."

"I can see that. I like it. I'll just be one more second. You get into bed and hold that thought."

As I settled onto the crisp, cool sheets of our king size bed, I watched Landon. He was so handsome—so strong. He had been on the crew team in college and still had the broad shoulders and strong fore-arms of a rower. Everyone was always telling me what an attractive couple we made, and looking at him in his boxers still made me melt. He walked toward me with his strong naked chest exposed and his dirty-blonde hair slightly rum-pled from undressing, looking at me with his clear blue eyes. I felt myself blushing, overcome by his subtle and even boyish sexuality.

"What do you want?" he asked, kneeling before me and placing his hand on my naked stomach. The closet door was still open, and I noticed the gold buckle of his belt gleaming on the tie rack.

"Spank me," I said, turning over onto my hands and knees, presenting my buttocks to him.

"Oh, is that what you want?" he replied. I felt his warm hand drop onto the left cheek of my ass.

"Do it again, but harder," I murmured. He raised his hand and smacked it back down with a firm pat.

"Get your belt," I suggested.

"No." He pulled his hand away from

my ass. I eased down onto my stomach and turned over.

"You asked me what I wanted, and that's what I want," I replied. He stood up from the bed and paced toward the door.

"Where are you going?"

"To get a glass of water," he said. His voice was cold. He'd never liked doing anything remotely kinky. It was always missionary position, basic blow jobs, or if he was feeling adventurous, standard cunnilingus. He would never venture anywhere near my ass. I was lucky if I tricked him into penetrating me doggy style.

"Come back," I pleaded. "I want your tongue inside me." He looked back at me with his big blue eyes and walked toward me. I edged my body to the side of the bed and spread my legs as wide as I could. He knelt down on the floor in front of me, gently parted the lips of my pussy with his hand, and started licking me lightly, making me wet. I looked up at the ceiling, moved by the feeling of his mouth against my cunt, and closed my eyes in ecstasy.

I felt his tongue working hard against my clitoris, dipping in and out of me while his finger pushed deeper and deeper inside me. I imagined what it would feel like to have the mysterious man from the bar pull his cock out of his trousers and force it inside me. As I moaned, Landon slid another finger inside me, dilating my pussy, dripping with cum. I pictured what it would be like to have my face pushed up against a wall. I wanted to come hard while he dominated me with his cock until he'd had his fill. As Landon's hand slid in and out of my wet cunt, I came hard, groaning loudly, and he slowly pulled away from me.

Chapter 2
Metro North

Landon had already left for work when I rolled over to check the time on my Rolex: it was almost noon. I rarely slept past 8 A.M. My head felt fuzzy, like I had taken a sleeping pill. Lethargic, I walked from my bedroom to the front hall. My bare feet seemed to drag across the smooth parquet floors. I retrieved my iPhone from the gold evening clutch

I had used the night before. The calling card was still nestled inside, its golden sheen casting a glow on the cream satin lining of my purse. So I hadn't dreamed it up after all. One Valencia Lane, Bedford, New York. Was it even a real place?

I quickly typed the address into Google Maps on my iPhone, still standing naked in the foyer, my bare skin chilled from the central AC. After a few seconds the little red flag popped up on the map. It was a real place, located near a small body of blue water. And it would only take an hour and a half to get there from my apartment if I caught the next Metro North train.

I went to the kitchen to pour myself a glass of water. As the cool glass chilled my fingers, I gazed out the window and down at the bustling midday traffic on Seventy-ninth Street. I could catch a cab and make it to the train station in Harlem in a matter of minutes. The thought was tempting. I looked down at my engagement ring and wedding band sparkling in the sunlight. Why would I go to Bedford? What was I expecting to find on Valencia Lane? I had a beautiful life and a husband who loved me.

In an attempt to distract myself from the gold calling card, I showered and dressed. It was another ninety-degree day outside, so I put on a pair of white crochet shorts and a simple white tank top. Unlike Annabelle, my breasts were modest B-cups, so I could go without a bra whenever clothing or the weather warranted it.

My agenda for the day was modest: pick up necessities at Citarella, the local gourmet market, yoga at four o'clock, and investigate photography classes that I could enroll in for the fall. Modeling had piqued my growing interest in photography, and I was addicted to the DSLR camera that Landon had given me on our first Christmas as a couple.

Stationing myself at the white marble kitchen countertop armed with my MacBook and a fresh espresso, I perused the Internet for appealing course options. Before I knew it I was searching "One Valencia Lane, Bedford, New York" instead. There were no images of it online. I would have to see it with my own eyes before the day was over.

×

The Metro North train screeched to a halt at Bedford Hills, and my heart raced in my chest. All of a sudden the reality of the outing struck me. I felt ashamed—like I was a little kid waiting in line to see Santa Claus at the mall, but old enough to know that he wasn't real.

"One Valencia Lane," I said to the cab driver.

"Valencia Lane?" he asked.

"Yes. Do you know it?"

"Nope. Never heard of it," he said, shaking his head. "And I've been driving people around Westchester County for forty years."

"That's strange," I said, pulling out my iPhone to give him directions. He drove for about fifteen minutes, beyond emerald green horse pastures and classic country homes with immaculate land-scaping.

"This is the Hollywood Hills of the East Coast," the taxi driver said. "We've got all kinds of celebrities and billion-aires living here. Ralph Lauren, Martha Stewart, Catherine Zeta-Jones and Mi-chael Douglas. They all live in Bedford."

"Wow," I replied, watching out the window as we turned onto an unmarked dirt road.

"I guess I never knew this was called Valencia Lane," he said.

"I think I'll walk the rest of the way," I told him, thinking that perhaps who-ever had invited me wanted me to arrive alone. "But if you don't mind, could you wait here for thirty minutes? I'll pay you now, and if I don't come back by four o'clock, you can just leave. I'm not sure yet how long this is going to take."

"No problem," he said. I handed him a hundred dollar bill and got out of the taxi. I walked for ten minutes up the narrow, densely wooded road. There were small clearings here and there with rocks stacked into formations as though they had been placed there ritualistically. The clearings were bordered by meticulously kept stone walls. It seemed that all the land was part of the same property. I noticed a few No Trespassing and Private Property signs tacked to trees.

Right as I was about to give up and turn back, the dirt road ended and became a formal driveway paved with gray cobblestones. The woods became less dense and were replaced with vibrant green lawn. An expansive Tudor-style house sat at the top of the drive, complete with several gables and a clock tower. It almost looked like a historic home from the Normandy countryside, but there was something eerily artificial about it—like it was a life-sized Playmobil mansion instead of a real house.

I felt odd just walking right up to the front door, and once I made it to the top of the driveway, I couldn't even tell where the front door was. There was no sign of any cars or life at all. In spite of its pristine condition, it seemed abandoned, or at least closed up for the season. All the shades were drawn, so I couldn't see into any of the windows. I knocked at the front door, rang the doorbell several times, but there was no answer. Circling to the back yard, I saw a long oval swimming pool surrounded by the kind of cypress trees that encircle those country houses in Provence. The pool wasn't covered, which suggested that someone was staying on the property.

I rang the doorbell at the back entrance. "Hello. Anybody home?" I called, ringing a few more times in vain and banging at the heavy nail-head-trimmed wood door.

Afraid that I might be abandoned by the cabbie, I gave up and hurried down the driveway. Where the cobblestones turned to dirt road, a large tree branch had fallen, obstructing the path. It hadn't been there a mere five minutes before, and it almost felt like a set-up. Suddenly

I had the impression that someone was watching me—someone who wanted me to pause at that exact spot.

I looked around, on alert now. Then I heard the sound of someone wailing nearby. I followed the noise deeper into the woods until the terrain sloped down sharply and revealed an amphitheater below. It had stone auditorium-style seating that was overgrown with moss and in the center of the circular stage I saw the source of the screams: a naked girl was bent over, her ass in the air and her hands fastened behind her back; she wore a collar that shackled her to a metal hook in the ground. But she wasn't crying out in pain. She was screaming with pleasure, as a half-naked man fucked her hard. I watched from above, like a diabetic gazing into a pastry shop.

The girl was no older than nineteen and her long blonde hair was plastered to her head in an elaborate nest of braids. Sweat dripped down her back and her milky skin gleamed in the sunlight. Her ass was red with welts and her face was flushed with excitement.

The man penetrating her was twice her age but unusually robust, with salt-and-pepper hair and a thick beard. He was bare-chested and dressed in dark jodhpurs with black leather boots. His chest muscles pulsed as he moved. I felt myself getting wet.

The man was on the verge of climaxing. He kept one hand on her ass, which he squeezed and slapped occasionally, and the other he used to hold her arms taut, pulling her body back toward him slightly. He grabbed her by the hair and pulled her lithe body up against his. He whispered something in her ear as he grabbed her breast, and then tongued her aggressively. After the kiss, he pushed her back down, hard, against the ground. He pushed her face against the earth with his boot and fucked her hard from behind, moving faster inside her. The girl cried out, gasping for breath, in a paroxysm of pleasure and pain. The man started to grunt and moan. Finally he pulled himself out, his foot still forcing her face into the ground. With one hand he squeezed and slapped her ripe, swollen ass, while with the other he yanked his swollen cock. He groaned as a thick stream of cum shot out of his dick and sprayed all over her cherry-ripe buttocks. At last he lifted his foot from her face and the girl collapsed onto the grass. Immediately, her lover turned around and retreated to the woods, leaving her tethered to the ground, writhing in ecstasy, her ass covered with his cum.

I started to tingle and burn, my entire body infused with heat from deep inside myself. I wanted more.

Suddenly I heard a rustle coming from the woods and a second man emerged, this one younger, with a tall lean build and curly blonde hair. Just like the last man, he was shirtless and dressed for riding.

As he entered the amphitheater, the girl looked up at him, a mix of fear and excitement written on her face.

"On your knees," he shouted, and she pulled herself up off the ground, waiting in anticipation for his next command.

He walked around her and released her hands from the ties behind her back. The girl immediately began rubbing her red wrists together in pain.

"Be still," the blonde man shouted sternly as he stood behind her. The girl stopped moving and stared in front of her, expressionless, on her knees.

The man walked around her slowly, examining her, until he was standing in front of her, his crotch level with her face.

The girl looked up at him, her mouth open, eager to take him into her mouth.

"Eyes down!" he shouted.

She looked back down as he started

massaging himself through his jodhpurs, his huge cock beginning to bulge inside his tight pants.

He walked around her again, slowly, still feeling himself.

"Bend over!" he barked.

The girl, obedient, kneeled on all fours.

The man unzipped his jodhpurs and pulled out an enormous erect cock, even bigger than the last, as he looked down at the girl's ass and cunt, which she displayed to him like an offering.

He pulled a riding crop out of his boots as he started tugging on his swollen dick. Slowly, still examining her closely, he started whipping the girl. The girl, who continued looking forward, began to yelp in pain.

"Silence!" he shouted as he kept whipping her. She tried to keep quiet, but occasionally a gasp or whimper would escape.

"I said silence!" he would say, whipping her harder to punish her for her disobedience, until her porcelain skin was crisscrossed with red marks.

I kept touching myself, my hand dripping with cum as I worked it in and out of my pussy. The sound of the riding crop cracking down on her ass took me over the top, and I had to cover my mouth with my free hand to keep from crying out in ecstasy as I came right as he entered her and she shrieked again.

I wiped my hand off with a nearby fern and slipped my panties back on. I could have stayed there all afternoon watching the voluptuous debauchery unfold, but my taxi was about to leave, and somehow I felt that I was trespassing on sacred property.

Back in the cab I sat silently and looked out the window at the verdant pastoral landscape, rubbing the gold card, the thick paper smooth between my fingertips.

"Did you get what you were looking for?" the cabbie asked me.

"Not yet," I replied.

×

That night Landon didn't come home until eleven. He undressed, kissed me on the lips, and fell right to sleep. I lay next to him for half an hour, unable to close my eyes. My whole body felt wired.

I tried to masturbate but felt uncomfortable with Landon next to me. His body was as rigid as a corpse. He always slept fast and hard, barely moving an inch throughout the night.

At midnight I slipped out of bed and headed to the study to work on editing my photos from our recent trip to Scotland. I noticed a little spill of redness at the bottom of our front door. Someone must have slipped something underneath it in the last hour, since Landon had returned home. I opened the door to find that it was actually a scarlet ribbon attached to a small black package.

Tingling with excitement and anxiety, I bent over to pick it up. The waxy black wrapping paper unfurled to reveal a heavy gold box. I opened it slowly, half afraid that something would pop out of it, or that there would be a bloody finger inside. But instead there was only a small gold note like the calling card from the night before. In the same antique typeface, it read: 78th & 5th.

I went to the study, hoping to jolt myself back to reality with images of my marital bliss in the verdant Scottish countryside. I opened the single white drawer of our chrome and glass desk. It was one of those cold, modernist pieces that Landon had picked out because he had grown up in a house full of chintz and antiques. His MacBook was safely in its place inside the drawer. He rarely used it, since he had a separate laptop for work. Sometimes when I couldn't sleep I would take it out and log into his Gmail account, hoping to find out his secrets. He had to have secrets, like everyone else, but more and more I felt like he was a blank slate, as bland as Wonder Bread. His emails were always to me regarding dinner plans, to his mother regarding travel plans, or to his squash buddies regarding match plans.

But tonight I was determined to find something, clicking around endlessly in his computer's files, videos, and downloads. I had placed the gold calling card in the desk drawer, but it kept flashing through my mind: *78th & 5th*. Was I too late? Had I already missed whatever it was that was going to take place that night? In the glow of the laptop, I kept clicking, and that's when I found a strange video file. I double clicked it and turned the volume way down. A pretty girl with long brown hair was sitting in her bedroom wearing only a pink lacy bra and terry cloth booty shorts. She looked no more than fifteen years old. Her puppy dog eyes stared at me as she said flirtatiously, "I want you." She giggled, flashing her straight white teeth. She was so young.

"What are you doing?" Landon was standing in the door frame with a stern look on his face. I slammed the computer shut.

"Nothing," I said. He crossed to grab the laptop from the desk in front of me.

"What were you looking at?" he asked. He was pissed at me, but at the same time he was sweating profusely (an anxious habit of his). Beads of sweat dripped from his fingers down the front of the aluminum laptop.

"I saw the video," I said, grinning. "I know your dirty little secret." I was relieved.

"What video?" he asked, pacing back and forth.

"The one of that cute girl," I replied. "Sweetie, it's not a big deal. So you like kiddy porn? All guys watch porn. It's nothing to be ashamed of."

"What are you talking about?" he stammered, sitting down on the sofa and opening the laptop to see the video on the screen. I went to sit next to him, and he had already deleted the file.

"I have no idea where that came from," he said, panic written across his face. He had never been a good actor.

"Relax," I said, touching his back. "I

think it's kind of sexy."

"No, it's not," he said. "I don't want to talk about this, because there's nothing to talk about. Why were you even using my computer? Where's yours?"

"In the kitchen," I said. "Calm down. Don't be pissed at me. I'm not upset with you. I just want to talk about it so that I can understand what you like. Clearly there are things you want that you're not telling me about."

"I'm not having this conversation right now, or ever," he fumed. He shut down the laptop, slammed it shut, and stood up to shove it back in the desk drawer. "I've had a very long day. I'm going back to bed. And you should do the same." I sat on the sofa and listened as he stormed back into the bedroom, shutting the door behind him.

He was like a child. It was infuriating! Instead of punishing him for having a penchant for webcam videos of underage girls, I was embracing it as a harmless fetish. And he would probably ignore me for days until he had sufficiently deluded himself into believing that we had both repressed the memory, like the good Puritans that we were.

I waited for fifteen minutes, until I knew he had fallen asleep, and then I went back to the desk and opened the drawer to retrieve the gold calling card. I wasn't going to sleep that night.

CHAPTER 3
S.D.

By the time I made it past the oversolicitous nighttime doorman and across Park Avenue toward Madison, I realized that I didn't have my purse, or even my cell phone. The adrenaline rush had made me operate on autopilot. I felt naked, but liberated, still clutching the gold card from the black package.

It was past midnight, and the city

streets were silent. Most of the Upper East Side was away all of August in the Hamptons. It felt deserted. I looked up at the Doris Duke mansion that presided over Fifth Avenue at the corner of Seventy-eighth Street, a gleaming marble beacon of the city's Golden Age.

Right in front of the building a black Rolls Royce Phantom stood motionless. It struck me as odd, because it was a rare car, especially in a custom matte finish, which made it appear even more ominous in the evening light. But as soon as I saw it I knew it was my ride to One Valencia Lane.

I recognized the driver's green uniform; the valets at the St. Regis were wearing the identical outfit the night before. He nodded at me without speaking, and I stepped into the extravagant vehicle, knowing that I couldn't turn back.

The car started moving, but I couldn't see out the windows because they were tinted from the inside. The buttery red leather upholstery was soft against my bare thighs. Next to me on the seat there was a costume with a card on top of it that read: Greta White. My name. I was surprised to see it there, but then realized that whoever was behind this plot probably knew everything about me—from my dress size to my Social Security number.

The costume was an elaborate satin dress that looked like something Marie Antoinette would have worn, only instead of pastel it was a deep scarlet, and instead of being floor-length it was barely long enough to cover my ass. It fit me snugly.

My breasts nearly popped out of the ruching around the plunging neckline. I wriggled into the matching lace garter belt and black thigh-highs, but whoever had arranged my outfit wanted my cunt to remain fully exposed. To finish off the sexy courtesan look, there was a pair of black Christian Louboutin pumps that I slipped onto my feet.

And then it hit me: I could die that night and no one would know. I had no cell phone or ID, and I was being transported by a faceless driver to a remote property on a nameless street. Or the car could have been heading somewhere else. Either way, I would be powerless. That's what made me tremble with terror and arousal simultaneously. The stranger from the St. Regis, or whoever the mastermind of One Valencia Lane was, knew exactly what I craved—knew my darkest erotic desires, things I had never told anyone, especially not my husband.

×

"Welcome to the Castle," the driver said as he opened my door and took my hand. I stepped out of the Phantom and found myself standing at the foot of the cobblestone driveway, looking up at the same Tudor mansion from earlier that day. But nighttime had transformed its phony Disney World quality. The façade was awash in spotlights and the house glowed red from within, suggesting the depraved activities inside.

Climbing the hill, I felt exposed by

my lack of panties and the shortness of my new dress. The evening breeze cooled my warm skin and tickled my loins. As I breathed in and out, the corset-style bodice constrained my torso, shrinking my already slight waist while causing my tits to swell like balloons.

As I approached the house, trance music pulsated through the air. The front door was wide open, so I ascended the stone stairs and walked into the grand wood-paneled entrance hall. The room was lit by recessed red lights in the high ceilings, which made me feel like I was passing through the gates of hell.

A valet greeted me with a silver platter with rows of pills in varying shapes and sizes like hors d'oeuvres at a cocktail party.

"Crystals, Hawks, Jellies, Lucies, Vallies," he said.

"No thanks," I replied. I didn't need any added stimulation. I was already wired.

"You may show yourself around," he told me.

I wandered down the hallway of the first floor, which was lined with an extensive collection of swords and suits of armor. They glimmered in the flickering light from the candlelit iron chandeliers.

At the first open door I peered inside to discover a woman strapped into an S&M contraption. She lay with her stomach flat across a leather cushion, her arms suspended in front of her by the weight of heavy metal chains and her legs splayed open by two metal bars shackled to her ankles. She looked like her body was stretched to its limit by the apparatus. Two men took turns fucking her in the ass and in the cunt while a third man forced himself into her mouth.

The walls were padded in dark green and purple velvet. When I glanced down at the floor I could see the vague reflection of my pussy in the black lacquer tiles. I hovered in the doorframe, unsure of what to do next.

"You must be Greta," a woman's voice murmured behind me.

"Yes," I replied, turning around to see a young black woman with full red lips and perfectly round breasts. She was wearing the same outfit as me, only hers was emerald green.

"Sir Dannlo is ready for you," she

said, turning to lead me back down the hall to the main foyer. As I followed her up the black and white checkered spiral staircase, my heart beat wildly in my chest. I felt like my whole world was about to be opened up. My fingers trembled as I steadied myself against the cold iron banister.

Who was Sir Dannlo and how had he found me? I wanted answers, but more than anything else I wanted to be fucked hard. I wanted to be possessed by someone until I couldn't bear it any longer. I wanted to be split in half.

×

Sir Dannlo's chamber reminded me of what I imagined Napoleon's bedroom must have been like: a gold canopy bed wide enough for an army of people to sleep on, a roaring fireplace tall enough to step inside of, and a lighting installation on the ceiling that simulated the night sky.

"Tina, you may serve the champagne now," a man said. The voice was velvety, masculine, and mischievous all at once. Standing in front of the fire, I looked into the corner of the room and made out the figure of a man seated in a tall wing chair. I tried to discern the features on his face, hoping I would finally be able to see the man from the St. Regis whose touch I couldn't stop thinking about. But Sir Dannlo remained faceless to me, sitting strategically away from the fireplace, ensconced in shadows.

"Do you know why you're here?" he

asked. Tina brought me a chilled flute of champagne. My finger turned white as I touched the frosty glass.

"I don't know," I replied, taking a sip, the crisp effervescence of the drink refreshing me. "A man gave me a card with this address on it. I was at the bar of the St. Regis with a girlfriend . . ."

"I know," he interrupted me.

"So it was you?" I asked him, edging closer, trying to get a glimpse of his facial features.

"Be careful what you assume," he said sternly. "The Castle is a unique place, as I'm sure you've figured out from our special way of doing things. I'm assuming that you haven't told anyone where you are right now, or that you took a little field trip this afternoon."

"No, Sir Dannlo," I replied.

"Everyone who comes here has an unfulfilled desire, a sexual fantasy that has haunted them, a well of emptiness inside them. And this place fills it up, like a watering hole in ancient Greece." His words sounded like riddles.

"But how did you find me?" I asked.

"Try not to ask so many questions," he said. "I think it's best if you take off your wedding rings. Don't you?"

I slid my finger over my diamond engagement ring and wedding band and Tina stepped toward me to take them. She dropped them down the slot between her ample cleavage and into her bustier.

"Will I get them back?" I asked.

"That all depends on you," Sir

Dannlo said. "Now, remove your dress and lie down on the bed."

I obeyed, pulling my dress up over my head and handing it to Tina. In my mesh nude bra and panties, my gartered stockings and my stilettos, I mounted the epically large bed and arranged myself on top of the plush white blanket. I waited for Sir Dannlo's instructions.

Tina emerged from a closet carrying a small metal object. As she approached me, I saw what looked like a sharp needle.

"Tina is a wonderfully talented tattoo artist," Sir Dannlo announced. "She will administer a design just above your pubic hair. It will be painful. You may want to squirm or cry out, but you are not to move a muscle. We don't want the mark she leaves to be ruined. We won't be strapping you down, so you'd better learn to relax into the pain."

Tina approached the bed holding the tattoo gun in her hand. I lay still, gazing up at the red satin canopy above me, as she leaned over me and covered my eyes with a tight black leather strap that blocked out even the slightest glimpse of light.

"The blindfold is so that you can't see me," Sir Dannlo said, his voice getting closer. "Delayed gratification is the nectar of the gods." I felt my pussy getting wet as I listened to his footsteps approaching the bed and smelled his familiar peppery cologne, the same cologne that I had smelled at the St. Regis.

"Because while Tina is tattooing you,"

he continued, "I will be putting something deep inside you. Now, spread your
legs like a good girl." I felt his large hands
touch my inner thighs. He was wearing
leather gloves. Slowly, he spread my legs
apart until my knees were by my side and
my pussy was wide open, a gaping hole
waiting to be fucked.

"Pass me the silver bullet, Tina,"
he commanded, his hands still pressed
against my inner thighs.

"Now," he paused, "you probably
haven't ever fucked something this size
before," he said. "So just open yourself
up to it."

I felt a cool piece of metal against my
clit. My whole pussy was pulsing with
desire and I felt my body tremble in a
state of ecstasy. I waited eagerly for him

to push the smooth, hard probe deeper inside me.

For a moment he teased me, rubbing the dildo back and forth against my greedy clit, lubricating the massive dildo with my already wet cunt. I wanted to beg him to fuck me with it, but I kept quiet. Then, spreading my legs even farther back, he began to force the metal inside me, slowly letting my pussy dilate, until it couldn't go any deeper. The strange combination of pain and pleasure overwhelmed me, and I felt as though I was on the verge of fainting.

Just then, I heard the buzz of the tattoo needle and felt a sharp prick in the patch of skin above my pelvis, just below my right hip. It was hard not to flinch as the needle forced its way in and out of my skin but I remembered Sir Dannlo's command and obeyed. With the dildo still deep inside me, Sir Dannlo began stroking my clitoris with his gloved fingers. I could feel the cum dripping out of my pussy uncontrollably and my feet begin to quiver as my whole body responded automatically to the pleasure and the pain. With one hand gliding over my clitoris, he began plunging the dildo in and out, in and out, faster and harder, until I could feel my cunt opening up wide to accept the giant metal shaft deeper. My body trembled uncontrollably as I fought the urge to thrust my hips against the enormous metal rod.

Then Sir Dannlo leaned down, his face close to mine. His cologne wafted over me and I felt his warm breath against my neck. "That's a good girl," he whispered in my ear. As he spoke, I felt myself begin to cum harder than ever before. My engorged pussy began to spasm, engulfing the dildo, releasing a final stream of fluid in an eruption of passion. Slowly, as I finished, Sir Dannlo slid the metal rod back out. The buzzing of the needle stopped and I heard footsteps walking away. I had forgotten all about the pain of the tattoo, but it was over. Tina was done.

I heard a door close, and could sense that Sir Dannlo was no longer in the room. His presence had been palpable, and his absence like a cold wind over my charged body. Tina leaned close to me and I felt her breath on my breasts. She smelled tart and juicy, like a ripe currant bursting with flavor. As she removed my blindfold, my eyes were flooded with warm, crackling firelight, but Sir Dannlo was gone.

"Take a look," Tina said. I leaned forward to see my tattoo for the first time: thick black letters, "S" and "D," in antique script with a circle around them.

"Sir Dannlo has branded you," Tina explained. "You're lucky. I can tell he really likes you. More than the others."

I lay back on the fur blanket, satisfied for the first time in many months.

Chapter 4
Balthazar

Stark sunlight flooded the bedroom and roused me from sleep. One of us had forgotten to close the shades the night before. My newly tattooed pelvis still tingled, and I reached down to make sure the Band-Aid hadn't fallen off in the night. I didn't want my husband to see it. My whole world had shifted in the space of a day. Ordinarily I would have been panicked by something like a tattoo of some stranger's initials. But everything seemed different since I had experienced the Castle. I felt complete knowing that I was under Sir Dannlo's watch. My marriage seemed a million miles away, even though Landon was asleep next to me. He hadn't even noticed I had been away for most of the night and slipped back into bed at six in the morning.

I watched Landon as he got out of bed with bleary eyes and rumpled hair. He was still half asleep and would be for at least an hour. He couldn't tell that I was watching him as he started in on his morning routine: do fifty push-ups, take a shower, shave, dress for work, consume a glass of orange juice and a cup of black coffee, kiss his wife, grab his worn leather attaché case, and leave. Sometimes he would sit and have breakfast with me, but usually he liked to sleep in and didn't have time for such indulgences as eggs and toast, let alone morning sex.

Imbued with a new feeling of wholeness and sensuality, I sneaked out of bed and into the living room where he was on his fortieth push-up. He couldn't see me as I slid my smooth naked body against his back, sprawling myself on top of him.

"What's this?" he asked, turning over and sitting up on the white carpet. Grabbing my torso in his strong hands, he lifted me up onto him so that I was seated in his lap. I could feel his penis bulge against my crotch as he kissed me tenderly on the lips. It was clear that he had already wiped away the memory of the kiddy porn debacle, writing it off as a benign disruption of his pristine sleep pattern.

"You look tired," he said.

"Not at all," I replied. I leaned in for another kiss and then, my lips against his ear, whispered, "I want you." I started to kiss his neck and then began to make my way down his broad chest, his defined abs, all the way down to his cock. He leaned back against the edge of the sofa as I lingered on his muscular stomach, looking up at him playfully as I teased him with my tongue.

I wanted him to force my head down and hold it there until I obeyed—until I took all of him in my mouth. But he just sat there, waiting politely for me to do as

I pleased. If I asked him to be rough with me, he wouldn't know what to do. He would think I was being weird, or creepy, and probably get up and say he needed to leave for work. All my attempts to encourage him to dominate me had been total failures. He was such a Boy Scout at heart.

I started licking the head of Landon's cock, still looking up at him with big, coquettish eyes. I was on my knees now, and Landon was beginning to moan with pleasure. He closed his eyes and leaned his head back against the couch.

"That feels amazing," he groaned, pulling my hair away from my face and gently gliding my head rhythmically up and down his cock. I slid my tongue up and down the shaft of his dick a few times then around the head, making his penis swell.

"I want you," he said, gazing down at me.

"Let me make you come," I murmured. I slid him deep inside my mouth until the tip of his cock pressed against the back of my throat, choking me. Closing my eyes, I imagined that it was Sir Dannlo's dick I was receiving. I pictured myself sucking him, my wrists bound tightly with thick leather straps. He would push my head down roughly until my lips were on his huge, throbbing cock, while Tina pushed the cold metal dildo into my pussy. I remembered the touch of his gloves as he parted my thighs, and imagined him gripping my head forcefully with his big hands, pushing my head down and stuffing my mouth with his cock. His thick, stiff penis would fill my tiny throat until I gasped and choked, unable to take in a single breath of air.

I could feel Landon getting close. His cock was pulsating slightly and he was moaning the way he does just before he comes. I sucked gently and then eased him deeper into my mouth, loosening my throat to receive his cum. I wanted him to ejaculate hard into my mouth, but at the last minute he pulled out. He finished by jerking himself off into his hand as I looked up at him with wide, expectant eyes. He would never dare to come in my mouth, or even on my face. But I craved to feel his thick, hot cum on my tongue and dribbling down my lips.

"Thank you," Landon said, smiling, wiping his cum onto his T-shirt.

"You're welcome," I replied, disappointed. Flopping myself back against the scratchy wool rug, I wished it were the supple fur blanket on Sir Dannlo's bed.

"Shoot, it's already seven-thirty," he said, hoisting himself off the floor and hurrying off toward the bathroom. "Sweetie, can you make me an espresso when you have a sec?"

"Sure." He didn't even notice my Band-Aid. Part of me wanted to rip it off and march into the shower to show him. I would tell him everything about my night at One Valencia Lane—that I was willing to give up everything and run off with Sir Dannlo if he offered.

I kept the Band-Aid on, peeled myself

off the floor, and walked into the kitchen. The silver espresso machine glinted in the sunlight, reminding me of the metal dildo that Sir Dannlo had used on me just a few hours before. The relaxed, postcoital glow that I had woken up with that morning had already worn off. The driver deposited me back at the corner of Seventy-eighth and Fifth at daybreak without a word. I had been left with no instructions from anyone except that I was not to utter a word about the Castle, not even to myself when I was alone in my apartment. That was the rule. Sir Dannlo had left me hanging.

×

I went about the rest of my day shell-shocked, but in a good way, as though nothing would be the same again. By six o'clock I had wandered the streets of Manhattan from the Upper East Side all the way down to the South Street Seaport, the city's honky-tonk tourist trap that had been obliterated by a hurricane and was being transformed into some mega hotel complex with a Chanel store and whatnot.

An ex-boyfriend had taken me to an adult circus there one night. It was a strange place—half creepy and half corny. But the show had haunted me. Under the glow of the red canopy, a female acrobat had glided through the air on a swing and then entwined herself so that her whole body was bound. Her milky white flesh crisscrossed by thick ropes, she was like an animal caught in a trap. Then her partner came onto the stage and hoisted himself up onto the seat of the swing below her. The muscles of his bare chest glistened in the eerie lights of the tent. Vulnerable, she dangled above him. I had wanted her to spread her legs and offer up her pussy to his mouth as he swung them both back and forth. The routine continued in a purely acrobatic manner instead of an erotic one. But I kept going back in my imagination to the circus for years to come. It had sparked something inside me. From then on, I craved more danger in my sex life, imagining myself as the female acrobat dangling from the ropes of a swing with her lover seated beneath her and her life dangling before her eyes.

As I stood on the pier, looking out at the view of Brooklyn, I felt a twinge of anxiety stirring in my stomach. What if I never saw Sir Dannlo again? What if I never had the chance to feel his cock deep inside me?

I wandered away from the seaport toward Wall Street. The Financial District looked like some kind of gray Emerald City. Its stone buildings shot up like the stalagmites I had seen in the caves of Bermuda while on vacation with Landon. As I descended into the crowded subway station, I felt flooded by an overwhelming sense of purpose. After months of aimlessness and anxiety about the future, I finally wanted something that was bigger than myself.

×

That night I was supposed to meet a friend at an art opening on the Bowery but she never showed up. I stood in front of Sperone Westwater Gallery admiring the building: some famous architect had designed it, and it looked like a tower of airy, luminous glass etched into a sinister black steel frame. A huge red box moved up and down like an elevator, connecting the floors of the gallery as a floating room. I imagined Sir Dannlo trapping me inside that red box to live as his slave. I would move from floor to floor without even knowing it—ignorant of the world around me but completely free for the first time in my life. I belonged to him now. I could feel it.

"See anything worth buying in there?" a familiar voice asked. I turned around to see Landon striding toward me. He looked so handsome in his navy linen suit and crisp white shirt. He had taken off his tie and unbuttoned the top buttons due to the extreme humidity.

"How did you find me here?" I asked.

"Let's just say, I have my sources," he replied with a grin, leaning in for a kiss. His lips were full and moist, and his breath smelled of cigar smoke, which always turned me on. It was an indulgence that he rarely permitted himself, but apparently he was feeling frisky that day. I was as shocked to see him surprising me at a gallery opening as he would have been to see me reading a law book. He was probably anxious that I would grill him about his previously unmentioned fetish for underage girls and was merely doing damage control.

"Want to skip out on the art and go

to Balthazar? I'd kill for some oysters." The ease with which he repressed things was almost sinister, but since I was racking up my own dirty little secrets, I was willing to play along. Balthazar was my favorite restaurant, but Landon usually hated going there, because it was "loud" and "touristy," he said. I felt suddenly jolted back to the start of our relationship when he would surprise me with a bouquet of peach-colored ranunculus and a bottle of Billecart-Salmon champagne of the same color.

"Okay," I said. He grabbed me by the hand and we walked along Bowery toward Spring Street.

"Where are your rings?" he asked, looking at my empty ring finger.

"I took them to the jeweler," I lied.

"I'm having them sized down slightly. They always felt a little loose. Now that I'm not racing around to go-sees, I finally have time to get to my to-do list." As we strolled down Bowery, the pink summer dusk slowly faded to purple. I floated through the warm, buttery air, my body still tingling with the voluptuous energy of the Castle.

Chapter 5
Cleopatra's Needle

The days that followed were like those spent waiting for test results. Sir Dannlo had left me in limbo. I had no idea if I would ever hear from him, or his entourage, again. In an attempt to distract myself from pangs of desire, I enrolled in a photography class and made a point to see friends if Landon didn't come home for dinner. Each time I left my apartment

I felt on edge—anxious that I would turn around to see Sir Dannlo's black Phantom trailing behind me as I walked along the sidewalk.

But after a few days had passed and no one came for me, I felt more anxious than ever. Had he dropped me? His network and resources were so far-reaching that he probably had access to my most private thoughts. Had he sensed my ambivalence and eliminated me from his roster of victims? Would I never get to feel his huge cock throbbing inside me? I had had a taste of his universe, and I would never be the same again. It was as though the tattoo needle had pricked my skin and infused my veins with a potent sexual energy I had never before experienced. I was insatiable, masturbating at least ten times a day, always thinking of Sir Dannlo.

×

One week after my trip to One Valencia Lane I got out of my photography class at ten o'clock and started making my way home from my photography class at the National Academy Museum, on Fifth Avenue. The chill of September had arrived within the space of forty-eight hours, so I was wearing tight J Brand jeans and a cropped black leather jacket over my t-shirt. I passed the bulbous white monstrosity of the Guggenheim, and became aware of someone's presence close behind me. Their footsteps were loud on the pavement. I kept walking at the same pace, and when I reached the corner of

Eighty-sixth Street I heard them stop behind me as I waited for the walk signal. There was no one else around. It was one of those rare moments in the city.

"Greta," the man intoned. It was Sir Dannlo's deep, mischievous voice. My whole body trembled with excitement. He put his gloved hand on my waist. "Don't turn around. It's better if we prolong the magic. Just take a stroll. Enjoy the evening. The Castle seems like an appropriate venue. Don't you agree?" It was as though he only spoke in royal pronouncements. But somehow it relaxed me.

"What?" I asked.

"You've been there many times before."

"I don't know what you mean," I said, shivering from the excitement of having him so close to me. I had never expected him to find me in the city, away from the ostentation of One Valencia Lane.

"Come on, Greta. The Castle. Think, Greta, think," he urged with playful eroticism. I racked my brain and finally figured it out: he meant Belvedere Castle, in Central Park.

I crossed Fifth Avenue and headed into the park. Sir Dannlo remained within a few feet of me. I could feel his energy and smell his clean, musky scent. With each knock of his shoes against the paved walkway, I felt more and more aroused. I had been touching myself almost once an hour for the past two days and felt as if I would burst at any minute. My body felt flooded, warmed with sexual excitement. There was no turning back.

I walked behind the Metropolitan Museum, which was lit up like a jewelry box in the dark. The anticipation was unbearable. Would I finally get the chance to feel Sir Dannlo deep inside me, or was this excursion just another opportunity for him to push me to my limits and leave me begging for more?

As I passed Cleopatra's Needle, I thought of Landon. He had always wanted to take me to Egypt to show me the pyramids. At that very moment I could have stayed on the path and wound back out of the park to Seventy-ninth Street and run home. The thought came and went in a split second. I headed under the bridge up the path next to Turtle Pond. The park was dark save for the pools of light from old-fashioned street lamps and the spotlights illuminating Belvedere Castle, making it look like a fortress from *Grimms' Fairy Tales*.

As I ascended the final walkway to the castle, the path changed from pavement to steps etched into the rocky boulders of the artificial mountain.

"Are you ready to have some real fun?" he asked, his voice laced with intrigue. I could feel myself getting wet. I wanted him to tie me up and make a mess of me. I wanted the masquerade to end and for him to reveal himself to me once and for all.

"Of course," I said, stepping up onto the platform at the foot of the castle.

"I think I know what you're in the mood for tonight," he said. "Some good old-fashioned debauchery." He moved toward me from behind, and I felt his gloved hands around my waist. The energy from his body electrified me. His words were playful, but his touch was commanding and precise.

He guided me to the parapet wall and pressed my torso against the cold gray stone of the balustrade. I looked down and watched him shackle each of my wrists. The shackles were so heavy that I couldn't lift my arms, so I kept them by my sides.

Suddenly, I felt a sharp blade slide down my back. It cut through both my leather jacket and my t-shirt and grazed my skin. Little beads of blood trickled from the wound and dripped down my naked skin.

The pain was exhilarating. Despite

being half-naked on a windy night, I felt like I was on fire. I could have turned my head at any time to see his face. I was almost positive that he wasn't wearing a mask to conceal himself, because no one on the street had looked twice at him. But I had to follow his instructions or risk losing him forever.

I hadn't noticed, but I had started to cry. Not out of sadness or even discomfort. But cold tears were pouring down my cheeks.

"Poor Greta White," he said, touching my face with his hands and feeling my tears. He had removed his gloves. His skin was smooth against my cheeks. He slid his fingers down my neck and gripped it tightly, making it hard for me to breathe. With his other hand he took the razor blade to my jeans and sliced the top of them down the middle between the pockets and then ripped them so that my ass was exposed. It dawned on me that we were in a public place and anyone could have walked by and seen us at any minute. He caressed my flesh with one hand as he continued to choke me with the other, pressing on my Adam's apple so that I was gasping for air. At that moment I would have done anything for him to fuck me.

I felt his stiff cock against my ass. He was rubbing it against my smooth skin. Pre-cum had already spurted into the crack between my butt cheeks. My pussy was aching for him. I could feel its juices dripping down my thighs.

Sir Dannlo started jerking himself

off. I could feel his hand gliding back and forth against his hard cock, the tip shoving up against my ass as he pleasured himself. And then I felt him shooting his warm, thick cum all over my butt cheeks and lower back. It dripped slowly down the backs of my legs.

I heard him zip up his pants, and then he freed my wrists from the shackles. The next thing I knew, he was gone. I turned around, half naked and covered in his cum. Feeling more vulnerable and submissive than ever before, I proceeded to touch the lips of my pussy, which was already drenched and ready to be penetrated. As I touched myself, I went over the last ten minutes in my mind, fantasizing that it was happening again—that Sir Dannlo was still there behind me, forcing his hard dick up against my back and ass—degrading me and using me to fulfill his darkest desires.

Within seconds, I felt my cunt pulsating as I orgasmed so hard that I couldn't help but let out a shriek of pleasure. I collapsed on the cold stone. I leaned back against the wall. That's when I saw it. Just a foot in front of me on the ground there was a small gold box. I reached forward and opened it to find a card with the following message etched on it: Tomorrow. Nine o'clock. KCB.

The location came to me instantly. It was obvious. KCB. The King Cole Bar, where I had first met Sir Dannlo. He was there on that night when I was having drinks with Annabelle. It had been his scent that had intoxicated me. He had dropped the first calling card on the table next to my cocktail.

In a matter of hours I would finally get to see his face and feel him penetrate me completely for the first time.

Chapter 6
Fountain

It was almost eleven o'clock at night by the time I peeled myself up off the cold stone ground at the foot of Belvedere Castle. My daze lifted, and I realized that I had nothing with which to cover myself. Sir Dannlo had sliced up my t-shirt, jacket, and jeans. There was no way that I could cross the park and walk back to my building with my clothes falling off and his dried cum covering my back. I picked up my tote bag from where Sir Dannlo had tossed it on the ground nearby, nervous that my camera had been damaged.

That's when I discovered a gray hoodie and black yoga pants neatly folded at the top of my purse. At first I thought they were just some things that Sir Dannlo had bought for me, but when I put them on I noticed a small rip on the cuff of the hoodie. They were my clothes. He, or one of his employees, had been in my apartment and selected these items from my closet. I shivered at the thought. Somehow it aroused me to imagine Sir Dannlo in my own bedroom, touching my panties and smelling my perfume bottles. But part of me was terrified that I had gotten myself too deeply entangled in the game. If Sir Dannlo had access to my house, then he had access to my husband.

Before I could think it through, a couple walked by and shot me a dirty look. They were on a romantic date, and they probably thought I was a prostitute.

"Late night shooting," I said, lifting up my camera to show them. They smiled back at me, reassured.

I grabbed my torn clothes and dumped them in a trashcan as I headed back down the steps. There were two missed calls from Landon on my cell phone, which meant that he was probably back from the office and wondering where I was. Not that he even cared. Aside from the one nice night we had had together at Balthazar, he was still the same. He thought of me as the woman he had married. But I would have been shocked if he ever asked me anything about my innermost thoughts, feelings, or desires. That's why our sex life was so tedious. He channeled his sexual energy toward anonymous webcam girls and refused to open up to me about the details of this untoward desire.

As I walked back through the park and passed Cleopatra's Needle for a second time, I couldn't help but wonder if he could change. Perhaps I could invite the pretty, adolescent-looking hostess from Balthazar to join us in our lovemaking.

I stepped out of Central Park and onto the corner of Seventy-ninth and Fifth. The crosstown traffic blazed by. I felt like I had woken up from a fantasy.

Five minutes later I was tucked back into my safe, pristine apartment. It felt strange knowing that Sir Dannlo had been inside it. I set my bag down on the credenza in the foyer and looked at myself in the gilt-frame mirror to make sure that I didn't have sex written all over my face.

"You're home," Landon said. He was sitting on the couch in the living room reading a contract. He didn't even look up to greet me.

"I'm going to jump in the shower," I said, crossing through the living room. "I went jogging in the park before my photography class and didn't have a chance to before."

"Okay, sweetie," he said, still not looking up from his work.

The hot water enveloped my chilled body like a sudden patch of sunlight. The cuts on my back from Sir Dannlo's blade were so superficial that my skin felt smooth as soon as the water washed off the dried blood.

Part of me was disappointed as I examined my back in the mirror after I had dried myself off. I wanted even more of a mark of him on my body, beyond the tattoo. I covered it with another bandage, though I contemplated leaving it exposed for Landon to see in all its inappropriate glory.

I slept restlessly, like a kid on the night before Christmas. When I did manage to close my eyes and doze off for an hour or so, I dreamt of Sir Dannlo sitting across from me at the King Cole

Bar, but when I woke up, I couldn't remember his face.

×

That night I spent two hours preparing myself for my big evening out, doing the full feminine line-up of exfoliants, masks, razor blades, lotions, perfume, blow dryer, and full make-up. I felt giddy and drank a Diet Coke, which only made me more so. The last time I had felt like that was the night of my first date with Landon.

When it came to selecting a proper outfit for the rather unorthodox occasion, I half assumed that Sir Dannlo would have deposited something on my doorstep that he had picked out for me. But when nothing had arrived at eight-thirty, I rushed to my closet and searched through my collection of dresses, settling on a strapless scarlet minidress made of raw silk. It cinched under my cleavage and made my breasts appear twice as large as they were.

As I walked into the bar at ten of nine, I felt like everyone was staring at me. Maybe my outfit was slightly over the top, what with the cat eyes, cherry red lips, blown-out hair, and sky-high gold pumps. I marched straight across the room and sat down at the center stool of the glowing chestnut bar. It was surprisingly slow and eerily quiet for a Thursday night.

"What can I get you, miss?" the bartender asked, placing a glass of ice water in front of me.

"Nothing for now," I responded. "I'm waiting for someone. Thanks." I kept peering behind me and scoping out the room, assuming that I would know Sir Dannlo's face as soon as I saw it.

Time passed at a glacial pace. I stared up at the iconic Maxfield Parrish mural behind the bar of Old King Cole seated on his throne. The more I stared at the grandiose medieval figures, the more they looked back at me, smirks on their face, as though they knew something that was happening right behind me.

"That's John Jacob Astor," the bartender said when he noticed my sudden fascination with the painting. "Yup. The famous millionaire. And that's his face up there on the throne."

"Oh," I replied.

"If you ask me, he looks like he's up to no good," the bartender said with a snicker. "And with all that money, he ended up sailing on the Titanic."

"What do you mean?" I asked.

"He went down with the ship."

"That's ironic, I guess," I said, looking down into my water glass at the ice cubes as they slowly melted.

"More water?"

"No, thanks."

I stood up from the bar and headed to the bathroom. My head throbbed from anticipation. I rushed down the back stairs of the hotel. The women's room was blocked off for cleaning, so I peered into the men's room. The huge marble bathroom was vacant. The gleaming urinals looked somchow untouched. Like sculptures. I stood in front of the mirror and roughly lifted the bottom of my dress, tearing the beautiful red silk in the process. The tattoo was still there.

I walked into the first stall to go pee. And that's when I noticed it. A black velvet blindfold dangled from the coat hook at the back of the stall door. I heard footsteps from a man's shoes. Sir Dannlo. I knew instantly.

"Greta," he said. "I certainly hope it's you and not some unfortunate fellow." He was so comical and light, as though counterbalancing his powerful physicality. I could see his Italian leather buckle shoes on the other side of the stall door. They stood like surreal emblems of the sheer eroticism of the man attached, tempting me with their proximity.

"Yes," I responded. "It's me." My heart pounded in my chest.

"Maybe this is a good time to disrobe, so to speak," he said. "And put on that lovely blindfold." I went ahead and slid my dress off but kept on the gold pumps so that I would match his height. I wrapped the soft material over my eyes. It felt cool and smooth against my skin.

"And now I suppose you can unlock the door if you like," he said. I felt in front of me for the knob and managed to open it. He walked inside the stall. I could feel his body just inches away from me. But I still had the blindfold on. He grabbed for my pussy and unzipped his pants. His strong hands overwhelmed my cunt.

"This is it," he said. "*Carpe diem*. Don't you think?"

"Yes," I stammered.

"Now, turn around like a good girl and put your hands against the wall." I bent over the toilet seat and grabbed for the cold marble wall to steady myself. Crammed in the tiny bathroom stall, I felt closer to him than ever. I spread my legs wide and prepared to receive his huge cock. As he filled me from behind, my whole body began to tremble and convulse. He entered me slowly but before long he began forcing himself roughly in and out, grabbing my tits and pinching my nipples until they were as stiff as his cock. The pleasure enveloped every inch of me, like a fast-acting drug.

I could feel his rock-hard cock getting even bigger and starting to throb with fresh cum. My pussy spasmed and I came harder than ever before. Just when I didn't think it was possible to go on any longer, his cum shot inside of me and I collapsed in a state of ecstasy. Still reeling with pleasure, my heart pounded in my chest. I ripped off the blindfold to see Sir Dannlo's face, but he was gone.

But I had had enough of waiting for directions on little gold cards. My wish to be dominated had been fulfilled. And all I wanted was to find out who he was and how he found me. I picked myself up off the floor and pulled my dress and pumps back on before dashing out of the restroom and up the stairs to the brightly lit lobby.

I approached a young male receptionist.

"Could I have my room key?" I asked.

"Yes, of course, madam," he replied. "What's the room number?"

"It's under the name Dannlo," I said.

"Oh, yes, of course," he chimed. Lucky for me, he was clearly new to the St. Regis, as the sight of a short skirt was still able to sway him from proper five-star-hotel guest confidentiality etiquette.

"Right, thanks," I said, grabbing the large, old-fashioned gold key from his sweaty palm.

×

The room was on the top floor of the hotel. I walked to the end of the hall and reached for the doorbell before I realized that I had been given the key to the presidential suite. I had read somewhere that the nightly price tag was some absurd amount like $20,000. Classical music emanated from behind the door. I decided not to ring the bell or even knock. I unlocked the door with my key, opening it slowly to find a crowd of at least thirty men and women all standing around the opulent living room watching as a young Asian boy played some morose piece of serious music on a black grand Steinway. Everyone was dressed for a ball at Versailles, only they weren't wearing clothes, only elaborate undergarments inspired by eighteenth-century French decadence—frilly thongs, revealing thigh-high tights, partial corsets—and the men were naked under their plush velvet robes. Some of them even wore crowns and powdered wigs. No one noticed as I slipped in through the front door and passed through the foyer to the back of the audience.

Once I was part of the crowd, I realized that Sir Dannlo's party guests weren't merely enjoying the concert—they were coupled off or in groups of three, fondling each other or servicing each other in a variety of sexual ways. The twenty-something girl next to me stood perfectly erect and watched the pianist while a large forty-something man fondled her ass and another girl knelt on the floor in front of her sucking her clit. The entire room was a scene of partially restrained debauchery. The longer the music played, and the closer I looked, the nastier the deeds became. One petite woman was being double-teamed by two strong thirty-something guys while another man dipped his huge cock in her mouth.

I scanned the sea of faces and bodies in vain, hoping that I would somehow know when I saw Sir Dannlo. And all of a sudden I saw a familiar face: Landon's. He was seated in the center of the room right in front of the piano in a gold throne-like chair while one very young and voluptuous blonde girl crouched before him and gave him head. I was too shocked to even feel any pangs of jealousy.

But then it dawned on me. Where was Sir Dannlo?

Dannlo?

I visualized the letters of his name and somehow my mind finally opened up: Landon *was* Sir Dannlo. Their names were anagrams. He had orchestrated this whole dark, perverted scheme and wanted to remain anonymous to me. Maybe that was part of the fantasy for him. As long as I thought he was someone else and he felt protected by the persona of Sir Dannlo, he could do whatever he wanted to me without shame or fear.

And who were all these people? His guests? It was hard enough to wrap my head around the concept that Landon was capable of doing any of the things that he had done to me as Sir Dannlo. But it was nearly impossible to believe that he had involved all these people in his twisted other life.

Then I looked around and recognized a few men from his law firm and a couple of his squash buddies. They probably enjoyed this little underworld as much as Landon did. But he was the master of ceremonies, and that rattled me to my core.

I crossed through the crowd, standing out like the uninvited guest that I was in my short red dress, and knelt in front of him next to the beautiful blonde girl. He saw me, and his face went white. But the music kept on playing, and I removed the girl's tiny pink corset so that I could stroke the soft skin of her ample breasts. She looked up from Landon's stiff cock and gave me an inviting smile. I leaned in and took her place sucking my hubsand's throbbing penis. After a few minutes I lifted my head up for air.

"It's okay, sweetie," I murmured. "We have nothing to be ashamed of."

"I love you," he leaned over and whispered in my ear. "I fucking love you."

It was as if somehow, for the first time in our relationship, we were seeing each other clearly, and joyously accepting what we saw. The possibilities for mutual pleasure were as infinite as our vivid imaginations.

ABOUT THE AUTHOR

Bettina Davis is a scholar of medieval studies and the occult. She studied at the Sorbonne and has taught at Bunker Hill Community College, Charlestown, MA. This is her first work of erotic fiction.

One Valencia Lane
is available as an enhanced ebook
with additional multimedia content for
Apple iBooks and Amazon Kindle

For more information, visit
www.badlands.com